OWEN THE ASTRONAUT

Level 6H

Written by Lucy George
Illustrated by Emma Foster

What is synthetic phonics?

Synthetic phonics teaches children to recognise the sounds of letters and to blend (synthesise) them together to make whole words.

Understanding sound/letter relationships gives children the confidence and ability to read unfamiliar words, without having to rely on memory or guesswork; this helps them to progress towards independent reading.

Did you know? Spoken English uses more than 40 speech sounds. Each sound is called a *phoneme*. Some phonemes relate to a single letter (d-o-g) and others to combinations of letters (sh-ar-p). When a phoneme is written down it is called a *grapheme*. Teaching these sounds, matching them to their written form and sounding out words for reading is the basis of synthetic phonics.

Consultant

I love reading phonics has been created in consultation with language expert Abigail Steel. She has a background in teaching and teacher training and is a respected expert in the field of synthetic phonics. Abigail Steel is a regular contributor to educational publications. Her international education consultancy supports parents and teachers in the promotion of literacy skills.

Reading tips

This book focuses on two sounds made with the letters ow: ou as in cow and oa as in blow.

Tricky words in this book

Any words in bold may have unusual spellings or are new and have not yet been introduced.

> ### Tricky words in this book:
>
> **mission position their colours pictures**

Extra ways to have fun with this book

After the reader has read the story, ask them questions about what they have just read:

Why did Owen and the other astronauts have to leave the black hole?

Can you remember two words that contain the different sounds shown by the letters ow?

3... 2... 1...
BLAST OFF!

A pronunciation guide

This grid contains the sounds used in the stories in levels 4, 5 and 6 and a guide on how to say them. /a/ represents the sounds made, rather than the letters in a word.

/ai/ as in game	/ai/ as in play/they	/ee/ as in leaf/these	/ee/ as in he
/igh/ as in kite/light	/igh/ as in find/sky	/oa/ as in home	/oa/ as in snow
/oa/ as in cold	/y+oo/ as in cube/music/new	long /oo/ as in flute/crew/blue	/oi/ as in boy
/er/ as in bird/hurt	/or/ as in snore/oar/door	/or/ as in dawn/sauce/walk	/e/ as in head
/e/ as in said/any	/ou/ as in cow	/u/ as in touch	/air/ as in hare/bear/there
/eer/ as in deer/here/cashier	/t/ as in tripped/skipped	/d/ as in rained	/j/ as in gent/gin/gym
/j/ as in barge/hedge	/s/ as in cent/circus/cyst	/s/ as in prince	/s/ as in house
/ch/ as in itch/catch	/w/ as in white	/h/ as in who	/r/ as in write/rhino

Sounds this story focuses on are highlighted in the grid.

/**f**/ as in phone	/**f**/ as in rough	/**ul**/ as in pencil/ hospital	/**z**/ as in fries/ cheese/breeze
/**n**/ as in knot/ gnome/engine	/**m**/ as in welcome /thumb/column	/**g**/ as in guitar/ghost	/**zh**/ as in vision/beige
/**k**/ as in chord	/**k**/ as in plaque/ bouquet	/**nk**/ as in uncle	/**ks**/ as in box/books/ ducks/cakes
/**a**/ and /**o**/ as in hat/what	/**e**/ and /**ee**/ as in bed/he	/**i**/ and /**igh**/ as in fin/find	/**o**/ and /**oa**/ as in hot/cold
/**u**/ and short /**oo**/ as in but/put	/**ee**/, /**e**/ and /**ai**/ as in eat/ bread/break	/**igh**/, /**ee**/ and /**e**/ as in tie/field/friend	/**ou**/ and /**oa**/ as in cow/blow
/**ou**/, /**oa**/ and /**oo**/ as in out/ shoulder/could	/**i**/ and /**ai**/ as in money/they	/**c**/ and /**s**/ as in cat/cent	/**y**/, /**igh**/ and /**i**/ as in yes/sky/myth
/**g**/ and /**j**/ as in got/giant	/**ch**/, /**c**/ and / **sh**/ as in chin/ school/chef	/**er**/, /**air**/ and /**eer**/ as in earth/bear/ears	/**u**/, /**ou**/ and /**oa**/ as in plough/dough

Be careful not to add an 'uh' sound to 's', 't', 'p', 'c', 'h', 'r', 'm', 'd', 'g', 'l', 'f' and 'b'. For example, say 'fff' not 'fuh' and 'sss' not 'suh'.

Owen the Astronaut is going on a **mission** to explore a black hole.

Its **position** is known, but what
lies inside is unknown...

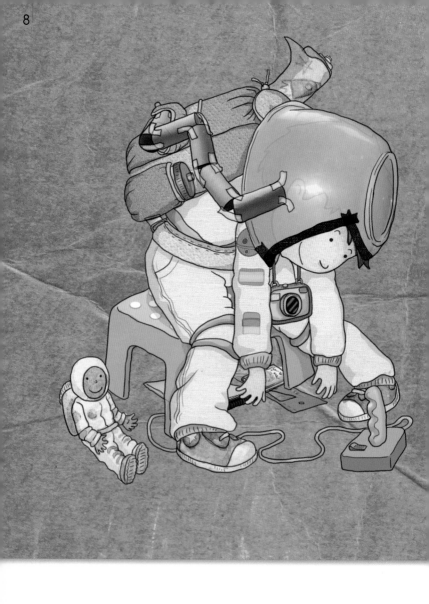

Owen stows his things below,
then he takes his seat.
He furrows his brow

as he looks at the controls.
There's a lot an astronaut
needs to know.

Outside the crowd cheers.
The engines growl and groan...
3...2...1... blast off!

Inside, Owen and the other astronauts are thrown back against **their** seats as they are blown into space!

Owen looks out of the
window and calculates how
far they have flown.

They have reached a great dark shadow, the black hole.

There is only a narrow entrance
to the black hole.

Owen aims the ship, and they are thrown in!

Inside the black hole is a tunnel.
They see swirling **colours** of red,
gold, brown and yellow.

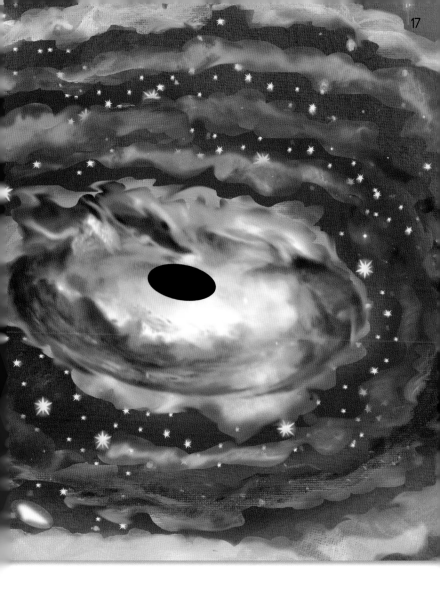

Owen takes a picture.
But then the tunnel grows
more narrow! Oh no!

Owen grabs the controls
and sharply turns the

spaceship around...
zooming for the exit!

They are thrown back again,
as they are blown out
of the black hole.

Phew!
Owen and his astronauts have
seen the unknown!

They look at the
amazing **pictures**,

and head for home,
far below!

OVER **48** TITLES IN SIX LEV

Abigail Steel recommends...

Some titles from Level 4

978-1-84898-582-7

978-1-84898-583-4

978-1-84898-585-8

Some titles from Level 5

978-1-84898-586-5

978-1-84898-587-2

978-1-84898-588-9

Other titles to enjoy from Level 6

978-1-84898-590-2

978-1-84898-591-9

978-1-84898-592-6

An Hachette UK Company
www.hachette.co.uk

Copyright © Octopus Publishing Group Ltd 2012
First published in Great Britain in 2012 by TickTock, an imprint of Octopus Publishing Group Ltd,
Endeavour House, 189 Shaftesbury Avenue, London WC2H 8JY.
www.octopusbooks.co.uk

ISBN 978 1 84898 593 3

Printed and bound in China
10 9 8 7 6 5 4 3 2 1